Super WHY

George and the Dragon

Based on the television series *Super WHY!*,
created by Angela C. Santomero, as seen on PBS KIDS

Text based on the script written by Sheila Dinsmore.

Adapted by Ellie O'Ryan   Cover Illustration by MJ Illustrations

Grosset & Dunlap

One day in Storybrook Village,
Whyatt gets an important message
on his Super-Duper Computer.
"Looks like Pig needs
our help," he says.

Pig tells Whyatt,
"Look! The giant stepped
on my new toy.
He is big and scary!
I want to get my toy back,
but I am afraid!"

Whyatt says,

"This is a super-big problem.

And a super-big problem

needs us, the Super Readers.

Calling all Super Readers!

To the Book Club!"

Whyatt, Pig, Red Riding Hood,
and Princess Pea meet
at the Book Club.
Whyatt says, "Together we will
solve Pig's problem."

Pig says, "The giant stepped on my toy. And I am scared to get it back! What can I do?"

9

Whyatt says,
"When we have a problem,
we look in a book!"

Princess Pea waves
her magic wand.
She says,
"Peas and carrots,
carrots and peas,
book come out,
please, please, please!"

A book flies off the shelf.
The title is
George and the Dragon.

Whyatt says,
"We need to jump into
this book to find the answer
to Pig's question.
It's time to transform!"

In a flash of stars,
the Super Readers
change into
super heroes.

Alpha Pig with Alphabet Power!

WONDER RED WITH WORD POWER!

Princess Presto with Spelling Power!

Super Why with the Power to Read!

They climb into their
Why Flyers and say,
"Super Readers . . . to the rescue!"
Then they fly into the book.

Princess Presto says,
"Presto! We're in the
George and the Dragon
book!"

Super Why says, "This book is about Knight George. He wants to rescue Princess Hope from a tower. But he is afraid. A scary dragon is keeping her there."

Princess Hope was stuck in a tower because of a scary dragon.

George was scared of the dragon.

Alpha Pig says,

"That's just like my problem.

I am scared of the giant,

just like George is scared

of the dragon.

We need to find George!"

The Super Readers find George.

Alpha Pig asks,

"Are you going to battle

the scary dragon?"

George says, "Yes, I am!
But I do not know
where the dragon is.
How will I find the dragon?"
asks George.

Alpha Pig . . . to the rescue!

Alpha Pig says, "With my
Amazing Alphabet Tools,
I can find the letters
in the word <u>dragon</u>
so we can get
to the dragon."

Alpha Pig says,
"Look! I see the letters
D-R-A-G-O-N.
That spells <u>dragon</u>.
The dragon must be
behind those trees!"

"ROAR!" goes the dragon.

"Lickety Letters!

We found the dragon!

He is very big

and very scary,"

says Alpha Pig.

"Princess Hope,
I will rescue you!"
yells George.
"ROAR!" goes the dragon.
"Ahhh!" cries George.
He is scared.

Princess Hope has an idea.
"If only we could make
the dragon fall asleep.
Then George could
get past the dragon!"

Princess Presto . . . to the rescue!

Princess Presto waves her
Magic Spelling Wand and says,
"I can spell the word <u>sleep</u>.
That will make the dragon sleep.
S-L-E-E-P. Presto!"
The dragon yawns . . .
and falls asleep.

One by one, everyone
tiptoes past the dragon.

They are trying to be very quiet.

"Shhhhh!" whispers Princess Presto.

They sneak past the dragon.

George cheers, "Hurray!"

The dragon wakes up.

"ROAR!"

George is scared.

Princess Hope says,

"Don't be scared, George!"

George says,

"But dragons scare me!

My story says so. See?

What can I do?"

The dragon scares George.

Super Why . . . to the rescue!

Super Why says,
"I can change this story
and save the day!"
He changes the sentence.
He switches the words
<u>George</u> and <u>the dragon</u>.
Zzzzap!

George scares the dragon.

George scares the dragon.

The new sentence says,

"George scares the dragon."

George yells,

"Boogely boogely boo!"

The dragon is scared.

He stops roaring.

Princess Hope says,
"Now you don't have
to be scared, George.
Just talk to the dragon."

George says, "Dragon,
let Princess Hope
out of the tower!"
And the dragon
goes away!

Princess Hope comes
down from the tower.
She says,
"Great job, George!"

George says, "Thank you
for helping me be brave."
Princess Hope says,
"You are welcome."

Super Why says,

"It's time for us to go.

Good-bye, George.

Good-bye, Princess."

The Super Readers hop
into their Why Flyers.
They fly out of the story
and back to the Book Club.

Pig says, "Now I know
what I have to do.
I have to be brave—
just like George was brave!"

Pig runs to the park.

He says, "Excuse me, Giant.

You are standing on my toy.

May I please have it back?"

The giant says, "I am sorry!
I did not mean to step on your toy!"
He gives the toy back to Pig.

Pig tells his friends,

"I was so brave.

I got my toy back

from the giant!"